MY FRIENDS

Copyright © 1989 by Chronicle Books.
All rights reserved. Published by Scholastic Inc., 555 Broadway,
New York, NY 10012, by arrangement with
Chronicle Books.
Printed in the U.S.A.
ISBN 0-590-48615-2

15 14 13 12   08   0 1 2/0

MY FRIENDS

by Taro Gomi

SCHOLASTIC INC.

New York   Toronto   London   Auckland   Sydney

I learned to walk from my friend the cat.

I learned to jump from my friend the dog.

I learned to climb from my friend
the monkey.

I learned to run from my friend
the horse.

10

I learned to march from my friend
the rooster.

I learned to nap from

my friend the crocodile.

I learned to smell the flowers
from my friend the butterfly.

I learned to hide from

my friend the rabbit.

I learned to explore the earth from

my friend the ant.

I learned to kick from my friend the gorilla.

21

I learned to watch the night sky
from my friend the owl.

I learned to sing from my friends the birds.

I learned to read from

my friends the books.

I learned to study from

my friends the teachers.

I learned to play from

my friends at school.

And I learned to love from a friend like you.